WINTER

AN ALPHABET ACROSTIC

WINTER

AN ALPHABET ACROSTIC

by Steven Schnur
Illustrated by Leslie Evans

CLARION BOOKS

New York

Clarion Books
a Houghton Mifflin Company imprint
215 Park Avenue South, New York, NY 10003
Text copyright © 2002 by Steven Schnur
Illustrations copyright © 2002 by Leslie Evans

The illustrations were executed in hand-colored linoleum blocks.
The type was set in 19-point Galliard.
Art direction and book design by Carol Goldenberg.

www.houghtonmifflinbooks.com

Printed in Singapore

Library of Congress Cataloging-in-Publication Data
Schnur, Steven.
Winter : an alphabet acrostic / by Steven Schnur ; illustrated by Leslie Evans.
p.   cm.
ISBN 0-618-02374-7
1. Winter—Juvenile literature. 2. Acrostics—Juvenile literature. [1. Winter. 2. Acrostics. 3. Alphabet.]
I. Evans, Leslie, ill. II. Title.
QB637.8.S36 2002
508.2—dc21
2001017358

TWP 10 9 8 7 6 5 4 3 2 1

At dawn, a thick
White frost covers the lawn
As the steaming
Kettle whistles
Everyone up.

Baskets of fresh bread
And muffins cool on the
Kitchen table in the
Early morning light.

Crystals
Of ice as delicate as
ʻ**L**ace ring the
Duck pond.

Does and fawns at the
Edge of the woods
Eye the frozen apples
Remaining in the orchard.

Even under caps, they
Ache and turn
Red in the
Stinging cold.

Flakes so
Light they drift
Upward
Rise like smoke before coming to
Rest in the
Yard.

Gusts of wind rattle the windows
As we sit by the fire
Matching puzzle pieces and
Eating popcorn.

Holly wreaths
On front doors,
Lighted menorahs
In living room windows,
Dinner guests, music,
And gifts at
Year's end.

In the north country,
Great blocks of ice
Lie heaped
On each
Other to make winter homes.

Just as the
Evening lights come on,
White flakes begin falling
Earthward, glittering
Like diamonds.

Knee-deep
In
New snow,
Dad carries a
Load of wood
Inside—thick logs for heat,
Narrow sticks to
Get the fire started.

Lamps glowing,
Ivory candles
Glittering,
Hearth fire blazing, stars
Twinkling.

Midnight falls, and
Over rooftops and bare
Oak trees a
Narrow crescent rises.

Nothing stirs
All night except
The wind, while deep
Under the snow chipmunks and
Rabbits dream of winter's
End.

One
Red and yellow
Cluster of flowers brightens the
Hothouse
In the
Dead of winter.

Pale moonbeams deep
In the woods light a circle of
Newly snow-covered
Evergreens that
Seem to dance.

Quickly we leap from
Under warm covers
Into sweaters and boots,
Late for school
This cold, snowy morning.

Racing along on
Ice skates, we feel our legs
Vibrate. Our
Eyes tear, our
Rushing breath smokes.

School is closed,
The trains have stopped,
Over two feet of snow cover the
Roads. Nothing
Moves.

The sun rises
Higher each day,
And as the ice begins to melt,
Water runs from the roof.

Unseen for
Nearly four months,
Dirt and grass begin to
Emerge as the snow
Recedes.

Vats of sap boil
In Uncle's backyard,
Slowly turning
Into maple syrup as we stir and
Taste.

Warm breezes blow
In from the south
Now that the cold
Dark days of winter are ending.

Xing the cloistered garden, we hear blue jays
Yammer and
Squawk in the budding
Trees.

Yes, we've had
Enough of winter's white,
And we long for the
Rich green of a
New season.

Zest,
Energy, and hope
Awaken with the bright
Light of spring.